THE CHRISTIAN HOUSEWIVES OF EAST NEW YORK:

Daughters of Eve Secrets Exposed

LINDA LEE MURRELL

THE CHRISTIAN HOUSEWIVES OF EAST NEW YORK
Daughters of Eve Secrets Exposed

Copyright © 2024 Linda Lee Murrell

Cover designer: Kimberly Gaffney
Editor: Jo Anne Meekins
Photo Credits: Antoinette Davis; Maurice Montgomery; and Rochelle Covington
Cover Photo Images: *Cast members of the book's theatrical production.* (L-R Standing) Linda Lee Murrell; Daphene Marshall; Hannah Phillips; Ericka Jenkins. (L-R Sitting) LaLa Scott; Muriel Anne Dean Ashby; Jauquette Greene.

Scripture references from various Holy Bible translations: English Standard Version (ESV); King James Version (KJV); Good News Translation (GNT); New International Version (NIV); New King James Version (NKJV); New Living Translation (NLT).

NOTE: *This is a work of fiction. Unless otherwise indicated, all the names, characters, businesses, places, events, and incidents in this book are the product of the author's imagination or used fictitiously. Any resemblance to actual persons, living or dead, or actual events is purely coincidental.*

Inspired 4 U Publications

Publisher@inspired4uministries.com
www.howtoselfpublishinexcellence.com

ISBN: 979-8-9859571-3-6

DEDICATION

I dedicate this book to God.
Thank you, Lord, for graciously bestowing the gift of
writing on me. I do not take it for granted or take any
credit because I know it is You using me.

"A sister is a gift to the heart, a friend to the spirit, a golden thread to the meaning of life."
— Isadora James

Table of Contents

"Be a good ancestor. Stand for something bigger than yourself. Add value to the Earth during your sojourn."

— Marian Wright Edelman

ACKNOWLEDGMENTS

I pay homage to my parents, Edith Theusdee McGowan and David Lee Murrell, and grandparents, Galloway and Robbie Lloyd, who live in the ancestral realm. My parents were hardworking individuals who took part in the Great Migration from the South and encouraged me to strive for the best. I got my work ethic from them and thank God for everything they instilled in me; it has gotten me far. I thank my mother for shipping me down south every summer to spend time with my Aunt Lillian and Uncle Lawrence, and my maternal grandmother, Robbie Lloyd. Those summers shaped my southern values. Also, much thanks to the rest of my family for your love and support.

Thank you, Prayer Partners, for keeping me lifted throughout each of my book writing and theatre projects; and those of you who consistently intercede on my behalf before the throne of grace.

Thank you, Church Family, for continually encouraging me in using my God-given gifts throughout these many years; I accept and embrace, "I am indeed a Storyteller!"

Thank you, Bishop Johnny Ray Youngblood and Rev. Dr. David K. Brawley, for guiding me through my Spiritual Journey and feeding my soul continuously.

Thank you, wonderful men *(Maurice Montgomery, Keir Nelson, Bruce Booker, John Johnson, Purnell Gates, Wilfred Green, Lorenzo Reynolds, Malik S. Canty, and Michael V. Robinson)* who ensured we had balance by contributing their apologies to Black Women in Chapter 8: The Apologia & Reconciliation.

And finally, thank you, Inspired 4 U Publications and Author Jo Anne Meekins, my publisher, encourager, and editor. I could not do this without your wisdom and direction.

FOREWORDS

Rev. Patricia Hodelin,
Exec. Asst. to Bishop Johnny Ray Youngblood,
Mount Pisgah Baptist Church

We all have stories to tell, and the *way* we tell them is as important as the stories themselves. A child's wonder can be satiated, an 'aha' moment awakened, truth defined, and healing fostered—all with the stroke of a pen and the words of a gifted storyteller.

Enter Linda Lee Murrell. Linda's unique gift lies in her ability to translate the complex tapestry of life into words that resonate with truth and profound insight. My first encounter with her was a decade ago at "The Youngblood Memoirs Think Tank," where her talents shone brightly under the mentorship of Bishop Johnny Ray Youngblood.

Linda's inaugural masterpiece, "The Surprise Witness: An Apologia for Adam and Eve," is not merely a book, it's a revelatory journey that reexamines one of the most pivotal stories in human history. With a keen eye for detail and a deep understanding of theological nuances, Linda dissects and reconstructs the Adam and Eve narrative, challenging conventional interpretations. Her ability to weave critical thinking with a compassionate understanding of human frailty offers readers a fresh lens through which to view this age-old tale. Her narrative sheds new light on themes of blame, forgiveness, and the inherent complexities of human nature, making it a groundbreaking work that resonates with the modern quest for understanding and redemption.

In her second literary feat, "The Youngblood Memoirs: The Man Who Built People, Not Buildings," Linda transcends the boundaries of traditional storytelling. This work is a profound homage to the influential Bishop Johnny Ray Youngblood, capturing the essence of his lifelong spiritual and community leadership. Linda meticulously gathered and presented the collective experiences of those touched by Bishop's life, creating a tapestry rich with personal growth, communal impact, and spiritual enlightenment. Her skill in capturing the nuances of each person's journey while maintaining the cohesive thread of Youngblood's overarching influence is a testament to her exceptional narrative skills.

My own extensive experience with women, from diverse walks of life, has been instrumental in my deep connection and identification with Linda's third publication. Her focus on the life journey of seven women, exploring the strength and significance of sisterhood, resonates profoundly with me. Having witnessed firsthand the intricate dynamics, challenges, and triumphs that women encounter. Her book is a mirror reflecting the multifaceted experiences of womanhood, capturing the resilience, empathy, and interconnectedness that define us.

Linda Lee Murrell is more than an author; she is a luminary who captures the heart of human experiences. Her books, especially her latest on sisterhood, echo the sentiments and realities that I, along with many others, have lived and felt. They are not just stories; they are reflections of our lives, reminding us of the indomitable spirit of sisterhood and the profound impact we have on each other's lives. Linda's works are an essential read for anyone seeking to understand the intricate weave of human relationships and the unyielding strength of women united.

* * *

Frances Bell Henry,
Chief Executive Officer,
Frank R. Bell Funeral Home

From the beginning of time, woman has presented herself as a mystery.

Have you ever questioned where woman comes from?

Was she created? Born? Evolved? Hatched?

Does she really come from man?

Whatever your belief, we know that woman is a life-giving force to keep the world populated.

In the dynamics of life, 'life-giving force' doesn't just mean an incubator to house the beginning of life, it also comes with the responsibility of resisting any death-promoting activities.

Linda Lee Murrell challenged us to examine male-female relationships with her first book "The Surprise Witness: An Apologia for Adam and Eve." In her current literary work,

"The Christian Housewives of East New York: Daughters of Eve Secrets Exposed," we get the full spectrum of sisterhood by way of triumphs and trials. The most "perfectly" framed lifestyles will get jilted by that insidious third party that starts out as the fly in the ointment, but eventually becomes the poisonous pot of soup which inches death into the camp, devouring its unsuspecting victims.

Linda, whom I've known for nearly four decades, rooted in the same church and eventually as an invited contributor to her compilation of Bishop Johnny Ray Youngblood's memoirs, has a passion for healing through stories.

As children, we learned some of our greatest lessons from stories which entertained while teaching on practical life situations. The tentacles of Village Life trickle from the elders to the 'young-uns'.

If you are a Baby-Boomer, a product of Gen X, Gen Y (Millennials) or Gen-Z, who understands and values that way of life even if you didn't appreciate it while it was being hammered into your upbringing, prepare to drink voraciously from the fountain of "The Christian Housewives of East New York" and quench your thirst, as the enemy's envious evil intent of the family unit presages you.

The enemy used Eve to get to God, so her daughters are even more vulnerable as an offshoot of the main vine.

Once again, Linda Lee Murrell takes on the role of griot, giving us a cross-generational view of what woman's true power looks like.

PREFACE

Can Anything Good Come Out of East New York?

In John 1:46 (NIV): Nathanael asks a similar question, *"Can anything good come from Nazareth?"* He also voices a criticism about Jesus' humble origins that is widely expressed particularly by members of the Judean elite, who believed that no Messiah or prophet could ever come from Galilee (see John 7:41-42, 52).

The History of East New York, Brooklyn

According to Wikipedia and City Neighborhoods-NYC, East New York is on the eastern border of Brooklyn, adjacent to Queens. To the north are its subsections of Cypress Hills and City Line. To the south are Starrett City and Jamaica Bay, while Canarsie and Brownsville are to the west. Tucked in the heart of this residential neighborhood is the subsection of New Lots.

East New York was founded as the Town of New Lots in the 1650s. It was annexed as the 26th Ward of the rapidly growing City of Brooklyn in 1886, and became part of New York City in 1898. During the latter part of the twentieth century, East New York came to be predominantly inhabited by African Americans and Latinos. Throughout the 20th century, the neighborhood experienced both economic growth and decline, with periods of urban decay and a rise in crime rates in the 1970s and 80s. However, East New

York underwent significant transformation with the development of new housing, retail spaces, and community initiatives to improve the residents' quality of life.

There was a time when this community was known as the murder capital of New York State, desolate and drug infested with abandoned buildings, prostitution, and no street signs; and if I may use my consecrated imagination, it was a modern-day Sodom and Gomorrah.

However, transformation occurred, like in the book of Nehemiah, when the ruinous condition of the city where his ancestors were buried troubled him. Nehemiah prayed to God for favor, then asked and received the king's permission to rebuild.

Many religious and political leaders took on the spirit and name of Nehemiah in rebuilding East New York. They joined to secure and transform long vacant, dilapidated land into "Nehemiah Houses"—property with newly built houses for first-time homeowners. God blessed me and hundreds of other residents to become owners of those single-family homes.

Can anything good come from East New York? Yes! Legendary Rapper, The Notorious B.I.G.; Award-Winning Actress Rosie Perez; Author and Licensed Social Worker Linda Lee Murrell; Assemblywoman Nikki Lucas; New York City Councilman Chris Banks; as well as some sisters in the theatrical production of this book.

You never know who is in our midst or about to be birthed. One of our children could discover the cure for cancer.

In God, we have unlimited potential no matter where we come from!

(Ephesians 4:32, ESV)

"Be kind to one another, tenderhearted,
forgiving one another, as God in Christ forgave you."

INTRODUCTION

Once upon a time, there were six women and the little girl who lives in each of them; they all came from humble beginnings and grew up in East New York. "The Christian Housewives of East New York: Daughters of Eve Secrets Exposed" looks at the evolution of these women since graduating from the "Journey to Womanhood" Rites of Passage Program under the tutelage of the community Queen Mother.

The women create a sisterhood bond that spans decades until exposed secrets and betrayals fracture their friendships, risking permanent damage. Amid their pain, they will discover how to redefine their relationships as they journey the path to forgiveness and reconciliation.

Spirit led me to create seven characters because the number seven (7) represents completeness. Every woman has a little girl within her, who we may not physically see, but is always there in the depth of every woman's soul; and when we don't heal that little girl, we become unhealthy grown women with little girl scars. We can try to mask the hurt, but the hurt will eventually reveal itself. It may come out in ways viewed as confrontational, explosive, over-reacting, or spiteful; and can create various instances of ruptured relationships with those closest to us.

Whatever phase of womanhood you're in is part of a lifelong journey; travel along on this journey of sisterhood and see if you find yourself anywhere in their story.

* * *

What Does the Number 7 Mean in the Bible?

In an article on 15 Degrees NE.com, Lucas Duxbury writes: "In the Bible, the number 7 means complete, or spiritual perfection. On the 7th day, God rested because His work was complete. The number 7 can also be about rest and wholeness, meaning that your rest comes from a sense of completing the work.

"When seeing the number 7 in your dreams, daily life, or a prophetic sign, there are two main interpretations:

1. **Something is Complete** — The Spirit of God may be trying to tell you a season is over, or a job is complete. There is a conclusion and perhaps it is time to close the book on that thing and move to the next thing.

2. **Rest** — Rest is a significant issue in the Bible and should not be overlooked. God rested when he had completed what he set out to complete. Jesus *became* our rest, going to the cross to carry our burden. Do you need rest?"

* * *

Housewives

According to Wikipedia: "A housewife (also known as a homemaker or a stay-at-home mother/mom/mum) is a woman whose role is running or managing her family's home

— housekeeping, which may include caring for her children; cleaning and maintaining the home; making, buying and/or mending clothes for the family; buying, cooking, and storing food for the family; buying goods that the family needs for everyday life; partially or solely managing the family budget and who is not employed outside the home (i.e., a *career woman*). The male equivalent is the househusband."

From our mothers' time until now, this definition of housewife has taken on a metamorphosis. Many women, as much as we would like, cannot afford the luxury of staying home because of economics; we end up forced to work in partnership with our men for a better quality of life.

And while there are different denominations of Christianity, a Christian is a believer and follower of Jesus Christ.

* * *

Help Meet/ Helpmate

Let's look at the word helpmate in relation to God's word, as in Genesis 2:18 (KJV): *"And the Lord God said, It is not good that the man should be alone; I will make him an help meet for him."*

Merriam Webster defines helpmate as "one who is a companion and helper; especially: wife."

The Hebrew word translated "helpmeet" is ezer, and it means "help" or "one who helps." The word occurs 21 times in the Old Testament, including twice in Genesis 2—first in verse 18, then again in verse 20 when Adam named the animals and could not find "a helpmeet comparable to him." In the other 19 appearances, *ezer* is never used in a negative sense. The term isn't used to speak of a sycophant, minion, or slave. Instead, it is used to describe great strength and support. — Richard and Sharon Phillips, Holding Hands, Holding Hearts, (Phillipsburg, NJ: Presbyterian and Reformed, 2006), 26-27.

I love the definition of helpmate as a woman being a great strength and support. There are many ways women can be help-mates, even if they aren't married. I learned to never compete with men because we, women, are man's helpers.

* * *

Yin and Yang

Yin and Yang relate to the created balance from the interacting feminine and masculine energy, respectively. In the beginning, God created Adam and Eve, equipped with male and female energy—BALANCE.

Dictionary.com describes the Yin and Yang as: "Two complementary principles of Chinese philosophy: Yin is negative, dark, and feminine; Yang is positive, bright, and masculine. Their interaction is thought to maintain the harmony of the universe and to influence everything within it."

* * *

We need mothers and fathers. However, when we don't have biological mothers and fathers present, God will stand in the gap; and is just to provide us with the gift of surrogate parents in many forms.

Chapter 1:
FATHER-DAUGHTER RELATIONSHIPS

Fathers, regardless of whether they're present, are the first person who teach little girls about men. Meet the women of our story and the fathers who influenced their lives.

* * *

Christiana

Christina means follower of Christ. I was always daddy's little girl; the favorite child, like in Genesis 37:3 (GNT): *³Jacob loved Joseph more than all his other sons, because he had been born to him when he was old.*

My Father was 45 years old when I was born; and my siblings were 15 or more years older than me. I believe daddy always thought he could finally get it right with me.

Growing up during the beginning of the Civil Rights Movement birthed revolution in my heart and soul, and in the rhythm of my feet. I was a brown-skinned, thin little girl who had extremely short hair, always smiled, and spent most of my time with my father when he worked in the boiler room. He was a building fireman who made sure the apartments in the projects of the New York City Housing Authority (NYCHA) got sufficient heat.

My daddy would stand me on a chair so I could reach the blackboard in the boiler room and pretend to be a teacher, writing out what I had learned in school. "You are the smartest, prettiest girl ever," my daddy would say with amazement.

He sometimes took me to White Castle for burgers and shopping once or twice; and although many families in the projects had black and white televisions, my father bought me a color TV—what a treat!

My father was my world, despite him being a womanizer, who did not always provide the maximum financial support for me. He would also promise my mother everything, but never gave her half of what he promised; yet she never spoke negatively about him or his limitations. When I got older and asked her why she never said anything bad about him, she said, "You saw the truth as you grew up, so there was no need for me to say anything that would ruin your relationship with him." Through it all, my father remained my hero; I continued to love him and always will.

I didn't realize it initially, but I chose men who were just like my father—hardworking womanizers; men who would make empty promises to me like he made to my mother. Then, I mistakenly rationalized that being with a light-skinned man would be different because my father was a dark chocolate handsome, muscular man. What was I thinking? Even though the outside package was different, the characteristics were still the same. I fell in love with all the counterfeits. It took me years to realize I attracted the same type of men repeatedly.

When my father began talking to me about the man I should date, he described men who differed from him. He'd look at me seriously and say: "Get a man with a good city job, and you get a good city job as well. It's a man's responsibility to take care of his family; the man should pay all the bills. Your money can go toward clothing for the children and savings."

Ironically, my mom told me the same thing: "If you go 50/50 and men have extra money, they will do other things with their money." 'Other things' meant spending it on other women.

In retrospect, my father did the best he could. I just wish he would have discussed with me what men like, what makes them happy, and how to always look my best to limit their eyes from wandering.

I thought being a good Christian girl, devoted to my husband, would make us both happy; but sadly, it seems the only one happy was me.

* * *

Griotta

Many call me the storyteller. Telling stories is my way of

hiding who I truly am. I grew up in Hollywood, CA because that's where my father booked most of his roles. He was an entertainer on many popular shows and word around town is he was one of the greatest Black Actors.

Although my father traveled often and was hardly home, we always lived in the most beautiful large homes; and never had an issue with clothing or money.

When I turned 13, my father moved us to Long Island because he was to film a new movie at a studio being built in New York. I mistakenly thought this meant he would finally be home more. I yearned for a relationship with my father, preferring his presence over all the fancy clothes, award shows, vacations, and other expensive things. He didn't need to spend any money on me; staying home to watch movies together or go to the park would have been enough!

I always made up false narratives about why he couldn't attend the father-daughter events at school. The stories I told turned my life into a fantasy and made me a master storyteller. However, I couldn't keep up with them, getting constantly lost in a world created by my highly overactive imagination. These tales swallowed whole my reality during therapy sessions, preventing me from receiving any real help.

To bridge the gap between me and the man who never had time for me, I became a variation of each character my father ever played; and because the only man I ever wanted a relationship with abandoned me for fame, I never desired a relationship with any other man.

Alina

My father loved and accepted me unconditionally. He was my protector against those who sought to make me into something I wasn't; including my mom, who often said, "Little girls are supposed to be feminine, wear dresses, and keep their legs closed." However, I always enjoyed playing sports and wearing baseball caps, baggy clothes, and sneakers; make-up was never a consideration. I struggled internally, forever at war with myself. The universe must have played a cruel trick—allowing me to be born a girl who felt like a boy trapped inside.

My father was my best friend. He taught me about cars and money management; and he enrolled me in karate class to learn self-defense. My spirit died the day he died, but resurrected when my mother enrolled me in the Rites of Passage Program with the community Queen Mother.

* * *

Amara

Amara means eternally lovely. My parents taught me how to receive love, love others, and focus on my looks. Dad was fine; he looked like a twin to former U.S. Rep. Adam Clayton Powell Jr., and mom resembled actress-singer Lena Horne. Inheriting their gorgeous genes afforded me *Pretty Privilege* and opened doors for me that some of my friends could not walk through.

I realized at a young age men desired me because of my beauty. Father often said, "A man always wants to be the envy of other men with a pretty woman on his arm." So, like my mother, I became the most delicious eye candy any man could ever want.

In our house, my father was the one who cooked, cleaned, and took us shopping for clothes. Mama would say: "Your daddy should take care of everything concerning the household; it takes a lot for me to be this beautiful."

Although I am a flirtatious, sexy dressing, lover, and connoisseur of all men, I have always been loyal to my sister-friends, regardless of what popular opinion might say.

* * *

Aaliyah

Our tradition teaches that a child lives out the meaning of their given name. Aaliyah means one who is off to success; and my parents worked together determinedly for me to be successful. They instructed me, from the age of two, to speak affirmations every morning after my prayers: "I Have A Purpose. I Will Live My Purpose. Everyone Connected To Me Has A Purpose. It Is My Destiny To Have A Purpose-Partner." It's amazing how reciting affirmations can transform your thoughts and elevate your self-worth to believe you are and can have what you say.

I grew up living a good life in the Hamptons, which was noticeably different from living in East New York. But my parents were adamant about me maintaining a connection to the East New York community, culture, and religious organization; so, our weekend visits to the community gave me the best of both worlds.

Looking from the outside in, most everyone would think I had it all. My purpose-partner Anthony grew up in Buckhead, an affluent neighborhood in Atlanta, GA, and planned out his career to include a seven-figure salary. We married and, along with my six-figure salary, took part in Atlanta's elite society. Yet—something was missing. Anthony was near perfect in everyone's eyes except mine. I came to realize he was exactly like my father—who I resented deep down.

When I got pregnant, I could not rejoice—it's complicated! My predicament will change the course of my life and relationship with my sisters in the Rites of Passage Program.

* * *

Yemaya

I am Yemaya. Can you imagine being teased in school because of your name? My parents defined my name and purpose soon after my conception. Initially, I didn't understand how sacred my name was—*Mother of All* aka *Queen of the Sea*. At age three, I saw *thousands of children surrounded by water*, and ran into their room to share my vision. It confirmed that naming me Yemaya aligned with my purpose.

My father was a professor who taught Black History at one of the most racist educational institutions in New York City; and both my parents were part of the Black Panthers' movement. Their involvement and my grandma's influence caused me to drum to a different beat, literally; and whenever I hear drums, I feel transported to the Motherland with the ancestors. My grandmother enrolled me in the 'Journey to Womanhood' Rites of Passage Program to afford me an opportunity to live out the spirit of the drums.

The movement and liberation of my people are in my soul; and I am a multidimensional woman who won't let anyone put me in a box. My life's mission is to advocate for and support Black women in attaining their highest maternal well-being to birth healthy babies.

I sacrificed love for many years, encountering many men solely satisfied with obtaining a six-figure job and a home in the suburbs. Finally, Martin entered my life. He was the manifestation of the love I desired; when I first saw him, he walked into the room like God had appointed him to be there.

I always figured I'd inevitably marry a carbon copy of my father; and like my dad, Martin was a professor of Black Studies. He was my king; perfect for me, or so I thought.

Chapter 2:
THE GATHERING

The sisterhood circle of housewives gathers at
Queen Mother Maya's home for her 90th birthday celebration.

Queen Mother is our mentor, who speaks life into us in ways no one else could. Born Maya Etta Foster, Queen Mother lives her life dedicated to her husband of 70 years, and to teaching the young people in the community of East New York. She uses her personal resources to educate children through reading programs, math tutoring, ritual dances, and cultural events.

When Queen Mother Maya was 60, she focused all her energies into the 'Journey to Womanhood' Rites of Passage Program she created for 16-21-year-old girls. Now, our aged and wise Queen Mother feels Spirit has confirmed that she's finished her assignment and it's time for her to move on. She prays that the former graduates of the program take on the responsibility of mentoring the next generation of young women to continue her legacy.

Who better to tell the story of our gathering? Yes, yours truly, Griotta, our group's storyteller. But don't pay attention to the ladies, who say, "Griotta can be a little ruthless with the truth." They only say that because they want other people at this birthday bash to think they are the Christian Women of the Year. However, I know about the deep dirt they trailing that's ready to catch them before they even get through the front door. Okay, let me rephrase—I'll call them *secrets* instead; *dirt* seems a little less harsh, right?

The funny thing about secrets—they come out at the most peculiar and inconvenient times. My sisters think no one will ever discover their secrets, but secret things done in the dark will always get exposed by the light. *"Whatever you have spoken in private will be public knowledge, and what you have whispered secretly behind closed doors will be broadcast far and wide for all to hear"* (Luke 12:3 TPT). Oh yeah, them thinking that they can keep their secrets undercover makes me want to laugh heartily and weep at the same time.

I am a woman of many hats that depict the energy I illuminate on each occasion. Today, I wear my multicolored hat so no one can tell what I'm truly feeling. My hats are my protection; they cover the hurt in my soul like veils, but when lifted, you can see the real me. Queen Mother is the only person who can and has lifted the veil of my hats.

* * *

Queen Mother Maya is a grand host who consistently provides a beautiful feast each time we gather. When I walked into the venue, the aroma of greens seasoned with smoked turkey, along with fried chicken, candied yams, and turnip greens permeated the atmosphere. There was even a pot of pig feet for that greedy Amara. Queen Mother also made a small cake for each of us. She knows our favorites and always spoils us at her annual Birthday Party, but insists that we never get her anything. However, this year, we have prepared a surprise presentation for her.

"Queen Mother, I know that ain't October London's song, 'Back to Your Place,' I hear playing." I don't know why it surprised me that this 90-year-old icon was up on the latest music. "His music reminds me of Marvin Gaye, and I love Marvin's music!" As I embraced her to dance, she tapped me playfully, saying, "Stop it," before bursting into silly laughter while swaying her hips to the beat. "You still got it, Queen Mother!" During that memorable moment, we laughed and hugged, like a genuine mother and daughter. "You're thinking about your mom, aren't you?" I immediately adjusted my hat even though I had never successfully hidden my feelings from her and, as usual, Queen Mother was correct. Yes, a fleeting thought of my mom, who I never really knew or hugged, had crossed my mind.

* * *

Here comes Amara, sashaying in with her Christian Louboutin four-inch red bottom heels, always looking and smelling glamorous. She hugged me while ensuring she mentioned her husband, Greg, had dropped her off. It was always the same: "Griotta, too bad you didn't get to see Greg. You know, he just got a new Mercedes-Benz."

As the other women showed up, we greeted each other, and prayed, laughed, danced, and shared. Have you ever known someone who had it all? Well, when God was giving out blessings, He gave Amara everything.

"Amara, how does it feel to be beautiful and desired by all men? And have a handsome husband who adores you and made sure you never had to work, even though you have a housekeeper and a nanny to care for your two children?"

We all light-heartedly talked about how we'd do anything to switch places with her. But despite Amara's abundance, she is loving and compassionate to all of us. I remember when she allowed me to stay with her for an entire month during a rough patch in my life.

"Yes, Amara has a wonderful life, but you all don't know the sacrifices she made to have that life," interjected Queen Mother, who always brought us back to reality whenever we drifted off into our fantasy world.

* * *

Alina arrived late as usual, dressed in her preferred baggy clothes with her nonchalant attitude, like she couldn't care less about being here. A beautiful, fully feminine looking woman always drops her off. Who does she think she's fooling and when is she going to be honest with us? I tried to open the lines of communication at the last gathering by asking her what her pronouns were. This happened right after I shared with the group how, as a teacher, I took a sensitivity training for discussing how youth would like to be identified. "What makes you think you know who I am?"

Alina lashed out immediately. "Pronouns don't define me!" You could have heard a pin drop from anywhere in the room. "Why y'all looking at me side-eyed?" I asked. "At least I speak my truth and don't pretend." "You wouldn't know the truth if it stared you in the face," Alina retorted. "None of you would know the truth!"

"If you all want to know Alina's truth, why not just ask her? Alina has been a straight shooter since childhood," Queen Mother said, addressing the entire group. "I can't do this today, Queen Mother. I'm going to call Michelle to come get me," Alina responded. "But first, can I go into the kitchen and fix a plate to go?" "Of course, beloved," Queen Mother said, as Alina walked away singing the Temptations' song, 'Smiling Faces.'

* * *

"Let's pray for Alina and all of us," Christiana said. But the looks we gave her prompted her to reconsider that suggestion, saying, "Well, I guess this may not be the best time?" "You got that right!" we all said in unison while laughing hysterically.

Christina, who had gotten married at 18 and is almost 60 now, shared she was expecting her first grandchild in a few months. Her oldest child was having a baby at 42 and Christina was peacock proud about finally becoming a grandmother.

Ted and Christina never seemed like an ideal match. Christina is a plain Jane—no make-up, drab clothes, and unshapely. However, she is the epitome of the Proverbs 31 woman. Christina devoted her life to serving her husband, her four children, and her church. Even though she had the option to be a stay-at-home wife, she committed to her part-time job in ministry; and she has always been a true sister in Christ.

We often told Christiana she was a fool since the time we noticed her husband Ted was showing signs of cheating. But Christina said she takes her vows, *'for better or for worse,'* to heart; and she's satisfied with having Ted be her first and only man.

I have my faults; but I'm aligned with God; and as an empath, I see and feel things others don't. It helps me as a storyteller. With that said, it tears me apart, not revealing to Christina the truth of what I see about her life. Queen Mother knows also but told me this wasn't the time for that revelation. In the meantime, Christina will carry on as the dutiful wife married to that counterfeit husband of hers.

* * *

Aaliyah is like an alternate version of Amara. She is an only child, who was born into a rich family and raised in the Hamptons. However, her parents made sure she maintained her connection to East New York.

Aaliyah was her daddy's rebellious princess; and although she loved her father, she swore never to marry anyone like him. So, she married Anthony, who was like a dream man to many women, with his seven-figure job, fabulous home, and glamorous vacations. Unfortunately, Anthony had been around Caucasians for so long, he had a disconnect with his own people.

Aaliyah told us she had something to share at our next gathering. Queen Mother Maya often cautioned her about procrastination, but Aaliyah must always have everything her own way. She's currently pregnant with her first child, even though she and Anthony separated over a year ago.

Aaliyah used to say Anthony was her purpose-partner, but since they're not together and she's pregnant, did she find a new purpose-partner? Did they get back together? Who's the baby's father?

We promised one another to adhere to a code and not keep secrets, but it seems secrets have become the core foundation of our group these days.

* * *

Now for Yemaya, the Angela Davis of the group. Sadness seems to permeate right through her soul, even with her joyous and nurturing spirit. I see the sorrow but also see an acceptance and awakening in her movements that lets me know everything is going to be alright.

Yemaya's parents knew her destiny when she was in the womb. Children, Revolution, and Community are in her DNA. She embraces her calling while many of us question God. Ironically, Yemaya—*the spiritual-mother of all children*—could not get pregnant with her husband Martin. Martin, the President of the New Black Panther Movement, told Yemaya, "The Creator didn't give us biological children because we are parents to the children of the movement."

Yemaya did not agree with his assessment and never got over him stating it. However, she continues to walk in her calling.

Alina's abrupt departure disappointed Yemaya because she wanted to discuss Martin's unilateral decision to be the sperm donor for Alina and her partner Michelle. We were all shocked and questioned why Alina had not shared this information with Yemaya or the rest of the group. Tears pooled in Yemaya's eyes as she shared how she had begged her husband, to no avail. "Martin, please let me freeze my eggs so you can inject your sperm and make it possible for us to have a child of our own."

* * *

As the evening ended, Queen Mother decreed: "One month from today, we will start a ritual with the Elders, and selected children and members of the community. After the Elders pray for us, we will shut-in and covenant to not have any more secrets or deception between us and within our space. My season as Queen Mother is ending on this earthly realm and I need someone or each one of you to step up. The children are crying out and they need all of you!"

Chapter 3:
SECRETS & BETRAYALS EXPOSED

The Value of a Friend
(Ecclesiastes 4:9-10, NKJV)

⁹Two are better than one,
Because they have a good reward for their labor.
¹⁰For if they fall, one will lift up his companion.
But woe to him who is alone when he falls,
For he has no one to help him up.

* * *

January is significantly special, being the first month at the start of a new year; and it's symbolically interesting that on this January day, it is raining steadily, as if cleansing away our sins, our deceit, and the dirty little secrets we keep.

We made a covenant in our sisterhood group to never keep secrets, to speak the truth in love, and to cherish our friendships above everything; and we declared, "If we get stuck, we will call on Queen Mother to help rescue us."

Although we vowed not to, we allowed the enemy—SHAME—into our souls; and it caused us to break our promises. We forgot God created us in His image, and provided the Ultimate Sacrifice that cleanses us from all sin and shame. Shame took root because we let demonized secrets creep into our souls. Those secrets birthed lies and deceitful actions, damaging the connection between our circle of sisters. We hurt each other in ways that were never addressed. But now, death is approaching Queen Mother Maya's doorstep, forcing us to reconcile and support her in making a peaceful transition when her time comes.

* * *

I knew today would be different. I'm usually the first person on the scene, but this time, everyone had arrived before me; and their early arrival prevented me from having my precious alone time with Queen Mother. As I enter the room, I empathically feel an uncomfortable energy in the atmosphere. Reluctantly looking into the eyes of my sisters, I sense the soul ties we share.

Soul ties usually originate between a man and a woman who've been sexually intimate; however, there can also be a soul tie between sisters that remains intact even after betrayal. The fact I consider myself an innocent member of the group convicts me of my guilt and deception. Remember—the storyteller can manipulate events and ensure they're seen as truth. In my false reality, I became the actor living the lie so long that I believed it was the truth!

My performance began immediately, as I smiled and

hugged each of them, unaware they saw right through my inauthentic spirit. In my discomfort, I walk away to get some food and a stiff drink to help me relax. Queen Mother, frail in body but strong in spirit, grabs me in mid-stride. Her forceful touch and fiery stare startle me. "No one will break bread or drink anything until we resolve this matter. You will not use any crutches or distractions until after this sister-circle is complete. Reconciliation must take place between the seven of y'all," she said firmly. "But Queen Mother, there are only six of us." "Griotta, my dear storyteller, use the gift God has given you," she gently instructed with glistening eyes.

What's happening to me? I wonder, crying uncontrollably, as I search the room until finally seeing her—the little girl. *What is she doing here? Who is she? Why has she come?* "Do any of you see her too?" "You always tripping. You'll do anything for attention. Every time we meet, you always seeing something no one else can see," Alina says while laughing in unison with the other sisters.

Christina stood, saying, "We've never respected or asked Griotta about what she sees." Still crying, I drop to my knees, "She is here, standing behind you all!" "Yes, she is here," Queen Mother intervenes. "She has always been around, but none of you acknowledge her. However, she lives inside each of you, whether or not you acknowledge her. Griotta can recognize her because she has the gift; she hears and sees what we don't and she can manifest what she sees into a physical being." Looking incredulously at Queen Mother and each other, the women laugh, except for Christina and

Griotta.

* * *

Queen Mother rises slowly, leaning on her cane, and walks over to stand in front of the women. Everyone sits like when they were in class. I sit Indian style on the floor to symbolize sitting at Queen Mother's feet.

"We don't have a lot of time. I've finished my assignment and my transition nears. The community of Elders have made preparations for the ceremony and are awaiting. But I cannot go in good faith knowing there is unfinished business here. I need the circle completed and to know there will be a successor from this sisterhood group who will continue my work. Our young women are dying, and they need the 'Daughters of Eve' to stand up. They need Christian housewives who don't fit the traditional mold and are women first. They need tough love, encouragement, hope, and all that good stuff. Most importantly, they need the women of the village to only speak the truth.

"God will hold us accountable for the lies we continue to tell. We put on airs with our red bottom shoes, fine clothing, great education, and stellar careers; but we are living lies, projecting what we want the world to see. Unmasking those lies can save our girls and young women, as well as save you, too. I cannot die in peace until we address these lies and secrets and put them to rest; never to awaken again unless it's needed to heal our community. Y'all are not getting any younger, so do it now before it's too late. Even though I know all your secrets, it's not my story to tell. Speak your truth and liberate yourself like I taught you. The clock is ticking, and we don't have all night. Who has the courage to go first?"

* * *

"As a voice for the children, I'll speak first," volunteered Yemaya. "I have felt broken for a long time, living my life pretending to be happy while making sure everyone else is okay. Even with the sisterhood, I say yes when I want to say no! I babysit your children so y'all can go on romantic vacations; and attend all your celebrations—weddings, graduations, proms, college bound parties—to not break our *sister circle*. But hell, the circle had already broken."

"In accepting the calling my parents and the community gave me to be the 'Mother of All Children,' I devoted my life to God, serving the children in the community, and teaching the children in the New Black Panthers' organization. Isn't it ironic, to be the mother of all children and yet repeatedly have one miscarriage after another, six at last count? How could God give me this calling and not bless my womb? And none of you ever asked me how I was doing, how I felt, or if I wanted to go out for a drink. When I planned a girl's weekend for all of us in Las Vegas, no one had time for me because you all were too busy with your lives.

"After several miscarriages, I wanted to try in vitro fertilization (IVF), but Martin did not support my decision, which drove us further apart. I knew we wouldn't last long together after the first year because something just seemed off. One person in this 'so called' sisterhood group knew what was happening, but never shared it with me. I kept asking you all, "What am I doing wrong as a wife for him not to love me anymore?" And how did y'all respond?— Silence then, and silence now!

"A brother that I went to school with shared with me that Martin is—I'm so angry I don't care about any pronouns or what is politically correct—Martin is GAY! My knight in shining armor would rather be with a man than be with me. I can't compete with that. I've had to join a support group with other women who have experienced the same thing. And what I can't get over is that YOU, Alina, are a snake who broke the sisterhood code, using Martin as a sperm donor for you and your partner Michelle! Now she's pregnant; how dare you! You should've used some other man's sperm? Why didn't you tell me? Why did I have to hear about it from someone else? You frequented the same bars with him and knew he was gay for years, but never told me. Why? Did you hate me that much?"

* * *

"It wasn't my story to tell, Yemaya. I never meant to hurt you. You are my sister. It has taken me 55 years to get comfortable and walk in my truth. Martin and I bonded over having the same struggle for many years; he is my friend also, Yemaya." "Of course you would protect him, Alina. Women always put men first."

"Don't do that, Yemaya!" Alina shouts as she jumps up. "You are both my friends; can't you imagine how torn I was? Let me just set the record straight and clarify that I love you,

Yemaya. I love you all, my sisters.

"For years, you all heard the rumors about me, yet never asked me about my truth. But before I go there—Yemaya, you may not understand it now, but I was protecting you. You, my sister, are one of the most beautiful and giving women I know. You deserve better! Not that anything was wrong with Martin; you two just shouldn't have gotten married. You both had a lot of similarities, but you were not compatible in other areas. Not to blame you, Yemaya, but we don't look at the signs, the red flags, the glaring warnings telling us to proceed with caution. Didn't you *ever* think it strange that 95 percent of Martin's friends are gay?"

"Looking back now, I should have known, but Martin also hung out with straight brothers from the organization, and I try not to judge. Alina, I feel you are blaming me for not knowing. However, Martin is one of the most masculine men I know."

"Men loving men has nothing to do with their masculinity but with who they love. We all have fallen into the stereotype of what a man loving a man looks like; however, therapy has shifted me into a different place. In all transparency, there are few Black men who will donate their sperm. But Martin was kind enough to do this for me and Michelle because of that shortage. I am sorry that I hurt you, Yemaya. Please know that I still love you and want to remain part of the sisterhood with you."

"I'll go next," Amara says with a sense of urgency: "I don't remember ever doing anything to hurt someone intentionally. But I can see I was not always there for you when you went through all your miscarriages, Yemaya. In my defense, I didn't know what to say. I felt a little guilty since I had four children of my own and didn't want you to feel uncomfortable. I was wrong."

"Amara, you didn't need to say anything. You're being there, letting me cry, holding my hand, hugging me, allowing me to scream and question God would have been enough. All I ever needed from any of you was your presence and a listening ear."

"I didn't think I could offer you anything because I was never pregnant; but I could have listened." "Yes, in-between storytelling," the women say to me before breaking into laughter simultaneously.

Queen Mother also laughed, saying: "It's so good to hear y'all laugh; don't take yourselves so seriously. Remember, I always tell you to listen to each other and also pay attention to what is not being said. Yemaya's silence spoke volumes about her pain; listen to the silence." As Yemaya collapses into sobs, the women rush over to embrace her in a group hug.

Speaking at Queen Mother Maya's encouragement, Amara continues: "My biggest hurt is being misunderstood by women. My mother taught me to always be beautiful and sexy because that will open doors. I never had a problem finding a job and as an Administrative Assistant, sitting at the front desk, men always fawned over me."

"IT'S CALLED PRETTY PRIVILEGE!" Alina rudely

interjects. "Similar to white privilege. Remember, during slavery, how the light-skinned slaves worked in the big house and slaves darker than a paper bag, worked in the field? You can't understand the struggle because you always lived a privileged life!"

"Amara, you better back up!" says Alina as Amara gets in her face. "Alina, you always have something negative to say. I can't help that I'm pretty, and men love me," Amara says, teary-eyed as she sits back down. "And hell, I love them too. I love them in all shades, whether they are dark as midnight, beige, or brown-skinned; I love them all." Griotta, looking puzzled, asks: "What the hell is beige?" Amara hugs her, saying, "Girl, that's the new description for Light-Skinned Brothers!"

"My beauty scares me because I fear people only love me because I'm aesthetically pleasing to the eye. But I am so much more and no one except my husband Greg seems to look past my outer appearance. I have a beautiful soul as well. Greg got to know my soul and the good qualities I offer. Where most men just wanted to get into my panties, Greg wanted and got to know the God in me; and that's why I love and married him. Women always say they wish they had my looks and sexiness to feel desirable, but sometimes feels more like a curse.

"You all frequently told me to just look pretty, as if it's my only asset. Often, I feel insecure whenever I'm around y'all because I'm the only one without a degree. I envy your high-paying jobs, careers, the vacations you take, and your independence."

"Being a career woman is not all it's cracked up to be," Yemaya says comfortingly. "You are more than beautiful. You're also an exceptional mother and a coach to your children, and a Proverbs 31 wife. I respect you and when I remarry, I will choose you as my matron of honor."

* * *

"As the Queen Mother, I am establishing some ground rules for us to implement. We will treat each other with respect; and Alina, no more bullying! I know you had to be tough to survive at 14, but you don't have to do that anymore."

Alina takes a breath before responding, "Alright, Queen Mother, but what about Griotta, always walking around in a daze like she does?"

"I am not in a daze; the Little Girl is here and has been present this whole time. Whenever someone speaks, she walks over and stands right in front of them; but it's like she's clear glass—even though she is standing in front of you, she doesn't block our view." The sisters look quizzically at Griotta, then at Queen Mother, and finally at each other.

* * *

"I have held my piece and now it's my turn to speak," says Christiana. "But before I speak, I want to thank God for my parents' legacy and wisdom in naming me. They raised me to know my purpose and devote my life to Christ, and I thank God for empowering me to serve Him.

"Ted, my husband of 35 years, is having an affair with a 'so-called' sister in this group. My apologies for thinking it was you, Amara, because of how Ted would look at you whenever we were all together. I thought little of it at first, since men are visual beings and will look; and who wouldn't rather look at you compared to me? I feel like Leah in the Bible, who Jacob married first, but really loved and desired her sister Rachel, who was very beautiful.

"The paralyzing pain I cannot get past is finding out that all of you knew about it and said nothing. And don't you dare say it wasn't your story to tell! If you check the Sisterhood Code, you'll realize some stories must be told to save a sister's life.

"While dusting the desk in Ted's basement man cave, I accidentally knocked over his large gold basket. Printed emails from ALT@gmail.com written to Ted fell out. Thinking back now, I doubt it was an accident? According to Queen Mother, there is no such thing as an accident.

"It's interesting that I found those emailed letters during a long holiday weekend when Ted was on a business trip last May; and our children were also away with the neighbors and their children for that Memorial Day Weekend. I was alone and able to read all seven letters, uninterrupted. The writer stated she felt torn because she was my good friend and part of the Rites of Passage Program. I knew it was one of my sister's here. The letters expressed how much she was in love with Ted and wanted him to leave me. Why would he keep those letters that he probably reread them multiple times?

"I automatically suspected Ted had betrayed me with Amara because of her beauty and sexiness; but things are not always as they seem. In the sixth letter, the writer spelled out that ALT@gmail.com stands for 'Aaliyah Loves Ted.'" The silence was deafening from that revelation, which seemed to suck all the air out of the room. "I shed enough tears and refuse to cry anymore."

"Aaliyah, you left your husband Anthony to have an affair with my Ted; and worse yet, you're pregnant with his baby. How could you? With all the men you could have, why attempt to steal my husband?

"We were looking forward to having our first grandchild and now he's having another child. Y'all may continue to call me a fool, but I am going to fight for my marriage; and Ted has agreed to fight also! I take my vows seriously and have always loved me some Ted. I should thank you, Aaliyah, because you brought Ted and me closer together and strengthened our marriage. We desire to raise your child as our own; and if you don't agree, we will co-parent the child with you instead. As a Christian, I must forgive you, but our relationship will never be the same. You betrayed my trust!

"I often wondered why none of you spoke up. Instead, you dropped hints that I didn't pick up on at our last gathering, suggesting I spend more time with Ted and watch who I let in my house. But, through it all, I learned a valuable lesson and can promise you I am a new Christiana from this day forward."

"So, I guess y'all consider me the worst woman of the

sisterhood now. Not to sound cruel, but *ish* happens! We all have sinned and done acts we're not proud of," Aaliyah proclaimed defensively. "There are no little sins; sin is sin, and we have all done sinful stuff. I am a very proud, privileged, and successful woman; but I have always committed to serve my community. What's wrong with wanting a man as successful as me and in alignment with my purpose?

"Christina, you were the last person I wanted to hurt. However, me and Ted are true soulmates. Anthony's focus is solely on making and maintaining seven figures. He was never concerned about how he could give back, only what the next level up would be for him. Ted and I started off as friends, conversing at the What's Happening Restaurant and Bar, where I would see him there with his fraternity brothers at least once a month. We connected on so many levels, talking for hours. I didn't see him as your husband; I only saw a man of substance who was everything I desired. The sex was an added connection; but I did not expect to get pregnant. Pregnancy was never a consideration, especially at 50-years-old.

"I will never forgive myself for hurting you this way; but I have to say—I will also never forget what Ted did for me and gave to me. Unfortunately, it cost me our friendship. In retrospect, it was not worth breaking the Sister Code or damaging our sister circle; and if it's any consolation, Ted made it clear he would never leave you and the children.

"I agree to co-parenting the baby with Ted and you.

Prayerfully, Christiana, I hope I can earn your trust again one day."

* * *

"As a storyteller since childhood, it is fitting I close out this session of telling our deepest and darkest truths out loud. You already know that I am the daughter of Raymond and Susan Parsons, and would always go into my imaginary world of playing various characters because it made me feel safe. It was something I learned from my father, the professional actor. The problem is that I never let people get to know who I really am.

"What you might not know is the stories I created and characters I played were about people I desired to be; and there were times I pretended to be each of you, my sisters, because of the greatness I've always seen in you.

"Queen Mother, the ancestors have spoken to me and given me a charge to become your successor. The ancestors will show me what more I need to do; and you will be the main one guiding me.

"Sisters, I cannot do this work alone; each one of you needs to take part in maintaining the success of the 'Journey to Womanhood' Rites of Passage Program! Remember, I am the one with the many hats of color (black, white, purple, and multicolor). My purple hat shows I have embraced my royalty, and so must you all.

"The Little Girl is Still Here; she hasn't gone anywhere. We hurt each other because we are all hurting little girls. God weeps to heal that little girl in each of us. Are you listening to His voice? When we women heal the little girls within ourselves, we can then be all God created us to be.

"Let us eat and celebrate our new beginnings!"

(Proverbs 18:24, NLT)

"There are "friends" who destroy each other,
but a real friend sticks closer than a brother."

Chapter 4:
THE HOMECOMING

"For nothing is secret that will not be revealed, nor anything hidden that will not be known and come to light." (Luke 8:17, NKJV)

Queen Mother Maya addresses the sisterhood: "Now that you all have exposed your secrets and betrayals that have poisoned this sister circle, it's time for me to speak some truths into your lives. You will find these truths familiar, but it's apparent each of you needs a reminder."

"The Spirit of God Represents Light! If you're involved in anything you feel you must hide or keep in the dark, then you need to ask yourself why? And although I don't advocate betraying a friend's confidence when they share a personal matter, you must consider if the secret is harmful to others or protecting someone from harm.

"Understand that secrets are powerful spiritual entities. Many unrevealed secrets that were buried with loved ones could have saved the loved ones left behind. Like keeping a secret that an uncle is a child molester leaves the children in the family and the community unprotected.

"Now, there are times you should keep your business to yourselves; for example, keep your positive and negative household and intimate matters between you and your husbands only, unless you intentionally share it with the purpose of helping someone else in a similar situation.

"Christina, your detailed conversations about Ted's outstanding qualities piqued Aaliyah's curiosity and interest in what was lacking in her relationship, causing her to yearn for what you had.

"Griotta's aunt raised her after her mother became pregnant at age 14. Griotta didn't discover her actual mother was her auntie's younger sister until her aunt was on her deathbed and her mother had been dead for ten years. All those wasted years keeping that secret and for what!?

"The secrets that this sisterhood kept allowed darkness to damage the bonds of friendship. In analyzing the demonic direction and destination of these secrets, I pose the following questions to each of you respectively to help gain the insightful retrospective answers that lie within your souls:

1. Aaliyah,
   - Why would you covet your sister's husband?
   - Did you ever consider if God intended for you and Ted to be together, you would have met and married him first?
   - If you believed it was a healthy and honorable relationship, why did you keep it a secret?

- What did you think and how did you feel when Ted told you he would never leave Christina and the kids?
- What did you think you meant to him?
- Do you believe there are women who men marry and those they just have fun with?
    - Which woman do you believe you are and why?
- What needs did you think you were fulfilling for him?
- Could you have been a blessing to Christiana as a supportive sister-friend by helping her in the areas she may have felt lacking?

Aaliyah, I assign you to reflect on these questions and answer them.

2. Christina,
    - How come you don't celebrate your beauty?
    - Why do you always cover up your body, dressing like you're living in the 1920s?
    - What's the real reason you got married?
    - What secrets have you been carrying your whole life?

3. My daughter Alina,
    - You are a special spirit in this physical realm, but why do you always seek control?
    - Why did you always feel a need to punish the sisterhood for not initially knowing that you are part of the LGBTQIA+ community?

- Why didn't you share with your sisters what it was like for you and teach them about the wonderful community you are part of?
- Why would you agree for Martin to be your IVF sperm donor, knowing he refused to allow Yemaya to have this procedure done on her?
- Why would you put your friendship with Martin over yours with Yemaya?

4. Yemaya,

   - Why did you ignore so many red flags?

   I'm only asking you this one question because your answers lie within it.

5. Amara,

   - How come you never try to do any of the things you dream about?
   - Why do you think you were the first one to know everyone's secret?

6. Griotta,

   - Why do you continue to be the chameleon of the sisterhood?
   - Will the real Griotta ever stand up?
   - Are you truly the storyteller of the group, or are you using someone else's narrative again?

"As you all answer these questions, consider the motives behind your actions; and know God will bless whatever you touch when you act with the right intentions."

Queen Mother Maya explains the healing ritual: "The Homecoming Ceremony will include two levels of Reconciliation — Level 1) **Apology** *for* the transgression; and Level 2) **Forgiveness** *of* the transgression. However, you will not worry yourself about receiving forgiveness from those you've hurt because you have no control over other people's actions or responses. Once you apologize and ask for forgiveness with a sincere and repentant heart, you have done your part; it is on the other person to accept and forgive or remain in their prison of unforgiveness. Also, understand that a person's forgiveness of you does not mean your relationship will be as it was before the transgression; it may never be the same and they may even decide to sever their relationship with you completely. What matters most today is that you Forgive Yourselves!

"Now, the reason I asked you to wear the outfit you wore for your Rights of Passage graduation ceremony and told you if it didn't fit, to wear a garment that was like the original outfit is because memory is powerful and wearing the garment will help transport you back to that time when we gathered with an unbreakable connectedness."

* * *

Without being told, all of us sisters gathered in a circle, placing Queen Mother Maya in the middle. Next, as the drums played, the attending community of children, men, and women walked over reverently, and surrounded us to take part in the phenomenon taking place.

Then, as if God was orchestrating our actions, each of

41

us in the sisterhood said, "I Apologize for All and Forgive Myself, I Apologize for All and Forgive Myself, I Apologize for All and Forgive Myself." That mantra became the benediction of the ceremony as we all hugged each other and our Queen Mother. The spirit of the *Little Girl* skipped around each of us, waved goodbye, and then slowly disappeared. I waved back and smiled as I watched her go.

Was it really a goodbye? No, this was not the end. The healing was just beginning.

* * *

La Trobe University states, "LGBTIQA+ is an evolving acronym that stands for lesbian, gay, bisexual, transgender, intersex, queer/questioning, asexual. Many other terms (such as non-binary and pansexual) that people use to describe their experiences of their gender, sexuality and physiological sex characteristics."

Chapter 5:
THE SISTERHOOD CODE

Queen Mother told us, "Mother-Daughter relationships are the root of how women initially interact with other women in their lives; and if the beginning of a mother-daughter relationship is traumatic, violent, abusive, condescending, or degrading, it will negatively set the path of the daughter's development in unhealthy ways."

She taught us about sisterhood because she came from seven generations of loyal women who practiced sisterhood principles. She believed the women in our communities must reach back and teach young girls these principles because they could help save our nation. When we, as Black Women, stop fighting each other and unite, we can become one of the major solutions to saving the Black Family.

* * *

GIRL CODE

Ellen Scott says, "'Girl Code' is the rules of being a woman, especially with regards to dating." Ms. Scott further states: "It's stuff like: you can't date your friend's ex., you also can't date your ex's friend. If you saw your friend's boyfriend cheating on them — you'd have to tell your friend. It's basically just that your loyalty is always with other women — that's what 'girl code' is supposed to be."

* * *

SISTERHOOD CODE

The Sisterhood Code is like the Girl Code. When we as women view sisterhood through a godly lens, we will fortify these rules in our souls and not break them. It will inspire mothers to teach the Sisterhood Code to their daughters and model the code in their lives as well.

1. **Be A Good Sister-Friend** — To attract good sister-friends, you need to be one. You accomplish that by first doing your own inner work. Deal with any trauma you may have experienced so that you can heal. If a sister hurt you, release that toxicity from your body with prayer, forgiveness, and therapy (if necessary). Your body keeps a record of the hurt and trauma you experience; let it go to be a whole woman again. In the words of Mrs. Michelle Obama, "When someone is cruel or acts like a bully, you don't stoop to their level. No, our motto is: 'When they go low, we go high'."

2. **Celebrate Your Sister-Friend's Achievements** — Clap, stand up, and support your sister-friend's dreams and accomplishments. Support her in one or more heartfelt ways, such as financial gifts, words of

encouragement, prayer, your presence, and ask her what type of support she may need. You can't fool God, so be your authentic self in celebrating her success. When one succeeds, we all succeed as a community because her success adds value to us all. If your sister-friend keeps getting blessed and your day hasn't come, WAIT YOUR TURN! Believe that there is nobody who can take anything away from you that is destined for you; and anyone who tries will fail!

My Story: Remember, I'm the storyteller and my life is an open book to bless others, sharing my mistakes and triumphs. I have worked in child protective services for 36 years; and even though I was more than qualified, the higher ups overlooked me for promotions for many years. Office politics played a role in my lack of advancement, like when I applied to get a managerial position someone recommended me for, but the Executive Leadership gave the position to a less qualified woman of a different ethnic group. In my disappointment, I told God that I would not apply anymore; and then I continued doing the superior work I've always done. When another opportunity for promotion came through a managerial test that rated applicants on education and experience, I scored 100%. They could not deny me this time because my experience and education spoke for itself. I got promoted to the same position they denied me in the prior year; and they demoted the woman from the other ethnic group because she had taken the wrong test.

Delay does not mean denial; wait your turn. What God has for you is for you!

3. **Respect Your Sister-Friend's Relationships — If** your sister-friend is married or has a significant other, always respect her in that relationship with her man. This rule also applies even if she's not your friend. That is a sisterhood rule that we all should honor. If you need a ride home, do not ask the mate directly; first, go ask the wife or girlfriend if it is okay, and then let her make the arrangements. I repeat, "You ask the sister; do not go to her husband or boyfriend!" I am a witness that your sister will thank you for the consideration because, unfortunately, this behavior is not the norm. Even if the man is your friend also, ask the sister first. Put yourself in her place. How would you like to be treated? Respect and maintain clear sisterhood boundaries.

4. **Your Sister-Friend's Ex IS NOT God's Choice for You —** Sisters do not date their sisters' husbands, boyfriends, or ex-boyfriends. More problems have occurred between sister-friends and sisterhood circles because of this frequently broken rule. The world would have us think there is a shortage of eligible men, but God has created abundance in the universe. Therefore, we do not have to operate from a low vibrational energy of dating our sisters' significant others; quality men are available. Sometimes, life circumstances and different seasons create missed connections, causing the right people to not get-together at a particular time. But, the goal is to always respect and follow the Sisterhood Code. When you

do, God can and will surprise you with what He'll bring your way.

5. **Be Grateful for Your Sisterhood Circle** — Be aware that some Sisterhoods *will not* invite you to sit at their tables. It may be because you and a particular sister in that circle don't click, or sometimes sisters will dislike you for reasons you don't know and can't control. Don't get discouraged; there are many tables to dine at. Celebrate and thank God for the sister circles that invite you to a seat at their tables or that you're already involved in. When you remain open with gratitude, the cuisine you receive from those tables will be the Feast of Sisterhood God Blesses you to enjoy!

6. **Keep Your Sister's Secrets** — Be her confidant, keeping her personal business to yourself. Don't even tell your best friend what another sister shared with you in confidence. Be the keeper of secrets and help support her through difficult times. Leslie Littlejohn says, "Be the woman who fixes another woman's crown without letting the world know it was crooked." There are Sister Acquaintances, Sister Besties, and Hi and Bye Sisters; if betrayed by any of them, act accordingly. Express your feelings to that sister before placing her in the suitable category of either restoration, distant dealings, or permanent removal; then heal from the betrayal, forgive, and move beyond it.

7. **Don't Speak Badly About a Sister** — Do not talk negatively about a sister or let a sister come to you speaking badly about another sister who is friends with you both. Encourage her to talk to the sister in question about whatever the issue is and work it out between themselves. What kind of sister-friend would you or I be if we let a sister trash talk another sister? Sister-friends should cover one another, hold each other accountable to the code, and be open and honest, in and out of each other's presence.

8. **Use Wisdom in Sharing Information That May Hurt Your Sister** — Seek God's guidance and pray, pray, pray and then, pray some more before telling your sister-friend something that may damage her spirit. For instance, if you saw your sister-friend's man allegedly cheating on her. Sometimes things are not as they seem; and you may not know all the facts. Is sharing this information going to help your sister-friend? Is this your first observation of an alleged indiscretion or multiple occurrences? Check your motives for sharing your suspicions; and proceed with caution. Some sister-friends end up angry with the bearer of the bad news. Let wisdom be your guide.

* * *

This Sisterhood Code is simple and can foster loyal lifelong sisterly friendships between women when they practice the principle and apply the rules. This book's storyline shows the damage that can occur when women don't follow the code.

For the women, who cannot heal your mother-daughter relationships on your own, I suggest you seek professional help and ask God to direct you to the right woman (an aunt, godmother, teacher, older sister, minister, or mentor) who can help you on your healing journey.

"Sisterhood is important because we are all we have to stand on. We have to stand near and by each other, pray for one another, and share the joys and the difficulties that women face in the world today. If we don't talk about it among ourselves, then we are made silent by the patriarchy, and that serves us no purpose."

— Ntozake Shange

Chapter 6:
QUEEN MOTHER'S TRANSITION

All the young girls and women from the Rites of Passage Program, close relatives, and a few select members of the community were at Queen Mother Maya's bedside. She appeared to be sleeping peacefully with a slight smile before whispering her last words: "Fear not! My God and the ancestors are also here with me; and I thank each of you who accompanied me on this earthly journey. Now, I'm ready for that heavenly journey awaiting me."

* * *

Our Queen Mother will live forever through this entire community of East New York as we continue her teachings about God, Black History, our bodies, and the many rituals she taught us. We were born to continue her legacy.

Through our differences, we have learned there is a greater purpose for us; and that we had to go through the pain, the secrets, and the deceit to be where we are today.

Job Well Done, Queen Mother! Rest in peace. Your assignment is complete.

* * *

Merriam Webster defines transition as: "passage from one state, stage, subject, or place to another: change a movement, development, or evolution from one form, stage, or style to another."

As we age, we see that our physical bodies are dying, however, our souls continue to be vibrant. The French philosopher Pierre Teilhard de Chardin states, "We are not human beings having a spiritual experience. We are spiritual beings having a human experience."

Foremost, we are spiritual. Our goal in life is to feed and develop our spirit by any means necessary. During our lifetime, the Spirit is the guiding force that helps us to navigate life. If we listen to Spirit, we won't go wrong. Have you ever met someone for the first time and felt in your spirit that something was not right with that person? The feeling you get when Spirit is speaking to you is hard to explain; however, you know it once you experience it.

We often say, *"Something told me."* In our evolution as spiritual beings, we learn to give Spirit the credit for that inkling or voice we call something. Jesus left us with the Comforter, also known as the Holy Spirt, who brings all things to our memory.

* * *

Will Queen Mother continue to live?

Is death the end or the beginning?

* * *

(Romans 6:23, ESV)

*"For the wages of sin is death, but the free gift of God
is eternal life in Christ Jesus our Lord."*

(John 11:25, NLT)

*"Jesus said unto her, I am the resurrection, and the life: he that
believeth in me, though he were dead, yet shall he live."*

(John 14:1-3, NLT)

*"Let not your heart be troubled: ye believe in God, believe also in me.
In my Father's house are many mansions: if it were not so, I would
have told you. I go to prepare a place for you. And if I go and prepare
a place for you, I will come again, and receive you unto myself; that
where I am, there ye may be also."*

"And I saw for the first time how, despite the isolation of our own lives, we are always connected to our ancestors; our bodies hold the memories of those who came before us, whether it is the features we inherit or a disposition that is etched into our soul."

— Alyson Richman

Chapter 7:
THE ANCESTRAL REALM

According to Wikipedia: "An ancestor, also known as a forefather, fore-elder, or a forebear, is a parent or the parent of an antecedent (i.e., a grandparent, great-grandparent, great-great-grandparent and so forth). Ancestor is any person from whom one is descended...."

Britannica states that in African cultures: "Ancestors also serve as mediators by providing access to spiritual guidance and power. Death is not a sufficient condition for becoming an ancestor. Only those who lived a full measure of life, cultivated moral values, and achieved social distinction attain this status."

This latter definition is more in alignment with my understanding and the teachings I received whereas, we cannot define everyone as an ancestor. The community gives ancestors their title and determines an ancestor's status by how they governed themselves while living in the physical realm. An ancestor is someone we should highly honor and respect because they contributed to their community and the world significantly.

I believe we should also consider an Elder as anyone who contributes positively to this world and lives to a ripe old age; and we should respect and honor them as well. This is my belief from what I've learned. Your belief may be different. However, the writer of Hebrews thought it important to pay homage to those who paved the way before us, as he did in chapter 11—The Hall of Faith. Many of the ancestors mentioned never lived to see the fulfillment of the promises, but they had hope and faith that those who came after them would experience all that they worked hard and sacrificed for.

Harriet Tubman helped hundreds of enslaved African descendants escape, believing for a time when all her people would be free, even if she wouldn't be alive when it occurred. She hoped for something more and better, without seeing that:

- The 44th President of the United States would be Barack Hussein Obama, the first Black Man to become President.

- The Civil Rights Act of 1964 would pass, prohibiting discrimination based on race, color, religion, sex, or national origin and race in hiring, promoting, and firing.

- Black descendants of African ancestors would teach at Harvard and other prestigious universities and organizations.

- The formerly segregated trains and buses would be driven by Black descendants who get paid well for their services.

- There would be a rise of 107 Historically Black Colleges and Universities (HBCU) to educate her descendants freely.

* * *

History.com states, "On March 7, 1965, when then-25-year-old activist John Lewis led over 600 marchers across the Edmund Pettus Bridge in Selma, Alabama and faced brutal attacks by oncoming state troopers, footage of the violence collectively shocked the nation and galvanized the fight against racial injustice." 'That 'Bloody Sunday' resulted in the mobilization of Congress to pass the Voting Rights Act, which President Johnson signed into law on August 6, 1965.

* * *

In my living room, I have "For Colored Only" and "Slave Auction" plaques on my wall. Many visitors have asked, "Why would you put that in your living room?" It's there to always remind me of what my ancestors went through, help me remain humble, and acknowledge that my position as a New York City Administrative Director of Social Services resulted from:

- Rosa Parks refusing to go to the back of the bus.

- Harriet Tubman and many abolitionists' efforts to free others from slave auctions and forced labor.

- Shirley Chisolm's political contributions and attempt to run for President in 1972, which paved the way for Barack Hussein Obama to run for and win the Presidency in 2008 and 2012, serving two terms successfully.

I never want to forget: Never Forget our Ancestors and Elders.

This is what the Community Queen Mother in this story taught and what we should teach our children!

* * *

Faith in Action (Hebrews 11:1-13, 39, NIV)

¹Now faith is confidence in what we hope for and assurance about what we do not see. ²This is what the ancients were commended for.

³By faith we understand that the universe was formed at God's command, so that what is seen was not made out of what was visible. ⁴By faith Abel brought God a better offering than Cain did. By faith he was commended as righteous, when God spoke well of his offerings. And by faith Abel still speaks, even though he is dead.

⁵By faith Enoch was taken from this life, so that he did not experience death: "He could not be found, because God had taken him away." For before he was taken, he was commended as one who pleased God. ⁶And without faith it is impossible to please God, because anyone who comes to him must believe that he exists and that he rewards those who earnestly seek him.

⁷By faith Noah, when warned about things not yet seen, in holy fear built an ark to save his family. By his faith he condemned the world and became heir of the righteousness that is in keeping with faith. ⁸By faith Abraham, when called to go to a place he would later receive as his inheritance, obeyed and went, even though he did not know where he was going. ⁹By faith he made his home in the promised land like a stranger in a foreign country; he lived in tents, as did Isaac and Jacob, who were heirs with him of the same promise. ¹⁰For he was looking forward to the city with foundations, whose architect and builder is God. ¹¹And by faith even Sarah, who was past childbearing age, was enabled to bear children because she considered him faithful who had made the promise. ¹²And so from this one man, and he as good as dead, came descendants as numerous as the stars in the sky and as countless as the sand on the seashore.

¹³All these people were still living by faith when they died. They did not receive the things promised; they only saw them and welcomed them from a distance, admitting that they were foreigners and strangers on earth. ¹⁴People who say such things show that they are looking for a country of their own. ¹⁵If they had been thinking of the country they had left, they would have had opportunity to return. ¹⁶Instead, they were longing for a better country—a heavenly one. Therefore God is not ashamed to be called their God, for he has prepared a city for them.

³⁹These were all commended for their faith, yet none of them received what had been promised, ⁴⁰since God had planned something better for us so that only together with us would they be made perfect.

(Matthew 18:15-16, NIV)

"15 If your brother or sister sins, go and point out their fault, just between the two of you. If they listen to you, you have won them over. 16 But if they will not listen, take one or two others along, so that 'every matter may be established by the testimony of two or three witnesses."

Chapter 8:
THE APOLOGIA & RECONCILIATION

Apologia

According to Collins Dictionary, "An apologia is a statement in which you defend something that you strongly believe in, for example, a way of life, a person's behavior, or a philosophy."

In her wisdom, Queen Mother of the Community knew it was key for us, as a community, to have our own Healing Ritual. We dedicate the babies that come from our wombs, so why not have a ritual where we also rededicate ourselves to each other and offer forgiveness for healing?

On December 31 of each year, the Rites of Passage Program includes an Apologia Ceremony. All the members of the community assemble at the East New York Church of the People on one accord, adorned in white; and there is a special reserved section for women who are pregnant. We place much emphasis on the expectant women because we learned that babies in the womb can hear and experience everything that is surrounding them, whether positive or negative. Many mothers are intentional to not argue or be around any negativity while expecting a child.

Healing Rituals are necessary because many of us are still hanging onto painful hurts and traumatic experiences that have prevented us from moving forward. We yearn to heal our souls, hoping for apologies that sometimes we get, but most times we don't. We must learn to regain our power and heal ourselves, independent of whether or not the perpetrator makes amends for their actions. Have you ever desired an apology?

* * *

It was a weekday night. I was watching television and thought it would be a relaxing evening. Through the telephone caller ID, I saw it was him; and my heart fluttered with anticipation of the special evening we would spend together. When I heard his voice, my body tingled thinking about the night of ecstasy awaiting me. He'd cook a wonderful meal using his excellent culinary skills and prepare smooth drinks, creating an enchanting vibe that opened me as a woman. Stolen moments, like tonight, were sporadic because I was just one of the many women in this man's Treasure Chest.

I had not evolved to the woman I am now, knowing the Sisterhood Code. It satisfied me just being with a man who was spiritual, educated, successful, fun, smart, financially secure, a lover of the arts, and an excellent lover, who had a great sense of humor and came from a good family. Through my limited world view, I did not realize I had developed a soul tie with this man.

My highly expected night of ecstasy resulted in the worse memory of our relationship history. The way our evening ended left me feeling unprotected; and began the downhill course of our relationship. We fell asleep after our lovemaking session until his phone rang and awakened us abruptly at 3:00 a.m. A woman from his Treasure Chest of women was calling to say she was on her way over; so he asked me to leave and called a cab for me. I dressed quickly and left into the dark wee hours. I knew God had His hand on me when the cab pulled up as I turned the corner. Thank you, Jesus, for rescuing me!

He later said, "Sorry for what happened." But I never felt I got an authentic apology. I thought about that incident many times after; however, through my healing process, I learned to forgive him.

I realized that the person God has for me would never treat me that way or put me in danger. Many horrible scenarios could have played out in the city that night; but God, in His love, offered me grace in my naivety. I needed to be healed before I was in a state of mind to accept his apology. In the book 'Feel the Fear and Do it Anyway,' author Susan Jeffers uses the quote, "When the student is ready, the teacher will appear."

* * *

Apologia has become a word I use in my books and dramatic presentations, believing if we first forgive the original man and woman (Adam and Eve) and then forgive ourselves, we can free ourselves from intentionally hurting each other. Forgiveness is the core message of my life's work and the key to healing relationships.

I always look at male-female relationships through a lens of forgiveness. My bottom line is the Black Man and Black Woman need each other. As wounded healers and people kissed by the sun, we have been through a great deal of oppression and adverse life situations. Counting on each other is the only antidote for us to be successful; each other is all we have.

Despite all the brutality that took place on the slave ships and plantations, we inherited the love and strength of our ancestors in our DNA. Unfortunately, however, our ancestors also transferred to us the disappointment, hurt, and betrayal they experienced.

It was strategic to tear Black Men and Black Women away from each other through the demonic intentionality of white supremacy. The Willie Lynch Letter, "The Making of a Slave," revealed the diabolical plan to separate Black men and women from each other and their children through enslavement.

* * *

Reconciliation

Ephesians 4:32 (NKJV) *32And be kind to one another,
tenderhearted, forgiving one another, even as
God in Christ forgave you.*

Below are some sincere apologies from Black Men to Black Women; and even though we, as women, have our own expectations of how and what we want their apologies to look and sound like, it is important that we listen to their voices with an open heart.

I fought back tears as I read through these apologies, feeling the authentic place of genuine love in which these men wrote and submitted them. There is no pretense, only a bared nakedness of themselves to us. Let the healing begin.

* * *

Our Kings Speak to Us

Black woman, I apologize and covenant with you for a positive transformation of my behavior from this day forward.

- Dear Black Woman, I apologize for being forgetful. *(Maurice Montgomery, Queens, NY)*

- I am sorry for not giving you the attention you deserved from me. *(Keir Nelson, Brooklyn, NY)*

- I apologize for the times that I couldn't protect you, and the times I let others disrespect you. *(Bruce Booker, Brooklyn, NY).*

- I apologize to my ex-wife for putting everything ahead of you. I should have made you my number one in life. I apologize for not being the man you deserved. *Explanation: When I got married, we couldn't have a honeymoon because I had been called to be a Police Officer with the New York City Police Department. My supervisor said I*

could go to the wedding, have our night together, but must report to work the next morning if I still wanted the job. I never cheated, but I was neglectful, giving everything to the Police Department. I realize my wife deserved more. She was a friend, confidant, and everything a man with good sense could want. I gave candy and flowers, but she deserved me, not just things.
(John Johnson aka J.J., Brooklyn, NY)

- I apologize for being aggressive and not understanding. I am so sorry for the lack of communication and the lack of not expressing my true self. I now look at what I can do better in my marriage. Young men must learn how to be compassionate and loving. Learn your mate's Love Language. We need to look at what we did in our past and learn what can we do better.
  (Purnell Gates, Grand Rapids, DT)

- I apologize for succumbing to the stereotypes and rumors that were aimed at us; and for not realizing and reacting positively to my godly potential and talents. I apologize for not recognizing the importance you had in my life and for not making you a part of my successes. I am sorry for not standing strong and steadfast in being the Strong Black man I was called to be. The list goes on....
  (Wilfred Green, Lubbock, TX)

- I apologize to Black women for having a lack of knowledge. In my opinion, the first thing we should have been taught is our true history and how to value a woman. The Black woman is the only woman who has the Eve gene that gives birth to all humanity. With that understanding, we should value the Black woman most and always respect her on all levels. The Black woman is the mother of life, and I apologize for not acknowledging it, not knowing it, and not treating her as such. In total transparency, my journey of loving, respecting, and appreciating a Black woman still isn't where it should be, but it's better than where it used to be. It's a forever learning journey I will continue to travel.

(Lorenzo Reynolds, Saginaw, MI)

- My dear sisters, as a Black man, I apologize for every time I thought you weren't enough. Not pretty enough. Not kind enough. Not good enough. I am sorry for believing the stereotype that you were just mean and angry. I apologize for not taking into consideration that I helped perpetuate that anger by not seeing you or your worth. I am so sorry for not trying to understand your plight.

  (Michael V. Robinson, Brooklyn, NY)

- I am sorry, Black Woman, for not being your King in times of need. Sorry for running away from my responsibilities when you needed me most.

  I know I have taken flight instead of standing and fighting for the preservation of my family.

  I am sorry, Black Woman, for the countless tears that I heaped upon you.

I am sorry for the cheating and mistreatments, and the non-communication of my fears.

I know that you have carried the burdens on your firm, gentle shoulders of raising our children by yourself, with little help from me.

I am sorry for being afraid of commitment, and I am sorry for making you believe you could fulfill all my needs, when even I can't.

(*Malik S. Canty aka Word Bird, Brooklyn, NY*)

* * *

A Women's Collective Apology
Love Letter to the Black Man

DISCLAIMER: Please note that not all sisters need to apologize for all the occurrences on this list. However, in the Spirit of Collective Sisterhood, even the innocent stand in the gap, holding a loving space for the guilty. We unite in our goal of healing the Black Family.

Black Man, we heal, letting go of the past to run into eternity with New Beginnings.

Black Man, we release the chains that restrained us from experiencing the fulfillment of being your Eve; and are ready to go, as in the song of October London, "Back to Your Place." The greatest of God's expectations for us is taking place, and it is better than any climax.

We apologize first for not forgiving ourselves for the mistakes we've made; and take full accountability for when we wronged you with mistrust and made you pay for what other Brothers did to us.

We apologize for using our words as weapons to castrate you because we couldn't win physically.

We apologize for seeing you as a paycheck and not encouraging you in your dreams and aspirations. Out of lack of faith, we wanted a steady paycheck and killed your spirit as an entrepreneur.

We apologize for not praying enough for you.

We apologize for using the children to get back at you.

We apologize for criticizing you for not providing us with that lifestyle in the 'Hamptons,' but never thanking you for what you did provide.

Let's start at a new beginning, as in the Garden, and realize WE NEED EACH OTHER!

* * *

(Genesis 2:15-18, 20b-22, NIV)

15The LORD God took the man and put him in the Garden of Eden to work it and take care of it. 16And the LORD God commanded the man, "You are free to eat from any tree in the garden; 17but you must not eat from the tree of the knowledge of good and evil, for when you eat from it you will certainly die."

18The LORD God said, "It is not good for the man to be alone. I will make a helper suitable for him. 20bBut for Adam no suitable helper was found. 21So the LORD God caused the man to fall into a deep sleep; and while he was sleeping, he took one of the man's ribs and then closed up the place with flesh. [22]*Then the* LORD *God made a woman from the rib he had taken out of the man, and he brought her to the man.*

ABOUT THE AUTHOR

Linda Lee Murrell has committed her life to the Ministry of Jesus Christ for 37 years. She is a prayer intercessor and part of the Leadership Team at the St. Paul Community Baptist Church under the leadership of Rev. Dr. David K. Brawley, Lead Pastor. Linda has facilitated workshops and has educated and trained new leaders.

Linda feels it is a privilege to be part of the Body of Christ, who implements 'church unusual' programming that transforms people's lives.

In addition, Linda is a licensed social worker, who has worked the past 36 years in City Government; and has learned significant professional and spiritual lessons in her purpose-filled family and community work. Linda is also looking forward to retirement in December 2024, to write and be a blessing to the East New York Community through the theatrical and community arts.

AUTHOR'S BOOKS

1. THE SURPRISE WITNESS: An Apologia for Adam and Eve

2. THE YOUNGBLOOD MEMOIRS: The Man Who Built People, Not Buildings

3. THE CHRISTIAN HOUSEWIVES OF EAST NEW YORK: Daughters of Eve Secrets Exposed

You Can Purchase All Books On Amazon

You can contact Linda at LLMurrell1095@gmail.com for any inquiries, updates, or comments; and follow her on:

Social Media Connections

- Facebook: @linda.l.murrell
- Instagram: @foxy1095
- LinkedIn: @linda-lee-murrell
- Threads: @foxy1095
- X (Twitter): @LindaLeeMurrell
- TikTok: @foxy109512

ANNOUNCEMENTS:

1. **Theatrical Production of The Christian Housewives of East New York** on Saturday, **July 20, 2024** @ 1:00 pm at Brownsville Heritage House, 581 Mother Gaston Blvd, Brooklyn, NY 11212.

2. **New Book Release Scheduled for January 2025**

"THE CHRISTIAN COUPLES OF EAST NEW YORK: Sons and Daughters of Adam and Eve."

Author Linda Lee Murrell's fourth book is part two of "The Christian Men and Women of East New York" book series; and the sequel to The Christian Housewives of East New York. Inside you'll meet the Christian men of East New York: Martin, Ted, Greg, Ricky (aka Santiago), Anthony, Joseph, and the community pastor; plus get to know Michelle, Alina's lover and wife.

As a bonus, the Christian housewives answer the questions that Queen Mother Maya posed in book 1, Chapter 3: Secrets & Betrayals Exposed, revealing an in-depth therapeutic view in to each of them.

As you interact with these characters, you will love some, hate others, and relate to all because it will be you or someone you knew. We are one, all connected, sharing many of the same aspects, similar tendencies, and stories.

Join us on this continuing journey and discover if you find yourself in the midst.

www.ingramcontent.com/pod-product-compliance
Lightning Source LLC
Chambersburg PA
CBHW060134260626
47160CB00005B/2099